P.Chr. Asbjørnsen
& Jørgen Moe

Fairy Tales from Norway

IVO CAPRINO'S
FAIRY TALE GROTTO

HUNDERFOSSEN
FAMILY PARK

ORIS

Foreword

– If you want to come along, climb aboard, says Askeladden. And now here is your chance! Climb aboard the fairy tale ship as we sail into Asbjørnsen and Moe's world of adventure! This is a fantasy world in which you as an adult will no doubt find delight, and which you can share with your children and grandchildren. In these days of stress and struggle, perhaps we need fairy tales more than ever.

In these ten stories you will meet many of the betterknown Norwegian fairy tale figures: the troll, the princess, the king, the smith, Butterball, and of course Espen Askeladden. In fairy tales the world is like we dream it should be: all ends well, Askeladden wins the kingdom, the bad people get their punishment, and the poor become rich. And fairy tales always side with the weak.

Do you think that trolls are wily, frightfully huge monsters? Wrong you are! Trolls are in fact both good and bad, naughty and nice. Trolls are both big and small, and they can have one or three or even nine heads! Most trolls are stupid and gullible. And just like people, they get scared when someone threatens them. They don't like the smell of Christian blood, but they can make a trip to church to invite people over for a feast.

Deep in the Norwegian forests, up in Norway's high mountains, and down in the low valleys, there are not only trolls. You will also find princesses and castles in the distance. But you have to work to get there, and you have to help people along the way. And then finally one day, you will find the kingdom waiting for you.

Norwegian fairy tale authors Asbjørnsen and Moe were inspired by the unique atmosphere of the Norwegian forests and the tranquil mountain meadows. They wanted to convey this feeling to others through their fairy tales and legends, and they succeeded. Jacob Grimm himself declared that Norwegian fairy tales were virtually unmatched by any other.

Asbjørnsen and Moe had the ability to listen. They immersed themselves in the fairy tales and shaped them so that they retained their artistic value. The fairy tales you will read here have come from deep in the living Norwegian folk tradition, and have been passed on in such a way that the reader is swept along on the ride.

In this book you will also meet the troll man himself, Ivo Caprino, the craftsman behind all the fairy tale figures shown in the photographs. You can see the figures for yourself in Caprino's Fairy Tale Grotto in Hunderfossen Family Park, just north of Lillehammer. There the Troll will bring you under his spell, as you embark on a voyage you will never forget!

Contents

Foreword	3
Askeladden and his Eating Match with the Troll	8
The Fox's Widow	13
The Three Billy Goats Gruff	19
Little Freddie and his Fiddle	22
The Seventh Father of the House	31
White Bear King Valemon	35
The Princess who Couldn't be Silenced	45
The Boy and the Devil	52
Askeladden and the Good Helpers	54
Butterball	66

Cover: The Hunder Troll, 14 m high

© ORIS FORLAG 1992
N – 1344 HASLUM, NORWAY

Printed by: Fabritius a.s.
English translation: Wendy Gabrielsen (The Fox's Widow), Diana L. Torrens
ISBN 82-7362-027-1

Askeladden and his Eating Match with the Troll

Once upon a time there was a farmer who had three sons. He was badly off and old and feeble, and the sons would not do any work.

The farm included a large, fine forest, and the father wanted his sons to cut timber in it, and try to get some of his debts paid off. At last he got them to listen to him, and the eldest son was to go out chopping first. When he got into the forest and began felling an old shaggy spruce, a great big troll came up to him.

– If you cut down my trees, I'll kill you! said the troll.

When the boy heard this, he threw down the axe and ran off home as fast as he could. He got there quite out of breath, and told what had happened to him, but the father said he was chicken-hearted. The trolls had never frightened him from felling trees when he was young, he said.

The next day the second son was to go, and the same thing happened to him. He had no sooner started to chop at the spruce when the troll came up and said:

– If you cut down my trees, I'll kill you!

The boy hardly dared look at him. He threw down the axe and took to his heels even faster than his brother had.

When he came home, the father became angry, and said that the trolls had never frightened him when he was young.

On the third day Askeladden wanted to set out.

– You indeed! said the two eldest. – You'll never manage it.

Why you've never even been outside the door!

Askeladden did not answer, but only asked for plenty of food to take with him. His mother had no curds, so she hung the cauldron over the fire to curdle a little cheese for him. This he placed in his knapsack, and then set out from home. When he had been felling trees for a while, the troll came up to him and said:

– If you cut down my trees, I'll kill you!

But the boy wasted no time. He ran into the forest for the cheese and squeezed it until the whey spurted out.

– If you don't be quiet, he shouted to the troll, – I'll squeeze you just as I'm squeezing the water out of this white stone!

– Oh dear, oh dear! Please spare me, said the troll, – and I'll help you!

Well, the boy would spare him, but only on that condition. Since the troll was good at felling trees, they managed to fell and cut up quite a few cords of wood by the end of the day. Towards evening the troll said: – You had better come home with me. It is nearer than to your place.

So the boy went home with him, and when they got there, the troll was to light the fire on the hearth, while the boy was to fetch the water for the porridge. But the two iron buckets that were there were so big and heavy that he was not even able to move them. So the boy said: – It is hardly worthwhile to take these thimbles with me. I'll go and fetch the whole well.

– Oh dear, no! said the troll. – I cannot lose my well. You make the fire, and I'll fetch the water.

When he came back with the water, they cooked up a huge pot of porridge.

– If it's okay with you, said the boy, – let's have an eating match.

– All right, said the troll, for he thought he could easily manage that.

So they sat down at the table, and the boy took his knapsack without the troll seeing it, and tied it in front of him, and managed to put more porridge in the knapsack than he ate himself. When the knapsack was full, he took his knife and cut a slit in it. The troll looked at him, but didn't say anything. When they had been eating a good while, the troll put down his spoon, and said:

– I can't eat any more.

– You must eat, answered the boy. – I'm scarcely half-way through. Do as I did, and cut a hole in your stomach, and then you can eat as much as you like.

– But I suppose it hurts one dreadfully? asked the troll.

– Oh, not that much, answered the boy.

So the troll did as the boy told him, and as you can easily imagine, that was the end of him. Then the boy took all the silver and gold in the mountain and went home. With that he could at least pay off some of his father's debts.

The Fox's Widow

Once upon a time there was a fox who lived with his wife deep in the forest in Fox Cottage. They were good friends and very happy together, as couples often are. One day, however, the fox got into the farmer's henhouse and gobbled up every single chicken, beak and all. Indeed he ate so much that he became ill and died. And however much the fox's widow wept and wailed, it made no difference; he was dead and that was that.

Now when he was good and buried and the wake was over, suitors started coming to visit the fox's widow. One Saturday evening there were three knocks on the cottage door. – Go and see who it is, Coshe, said the widow; she had a maid called Coshe who was a cat. When the maid opened the door, there was a bear standing on the doorstep. – Good evening, said the bear.

– Good evening to you, too, said Coshe.

– Is the fox's widow at home this evening? he asked.

– She's sitting inside, said the maid.

– What is the widow doing this evening,
   Is she merry or is she grieving? asked the bear.

– She's mourning because her dear husband is dead
   And crying so much her nose is quite red,
      she doesn't know which way to turn, said the cat.

– Tell her she only need turn to me
   And I will soon turn her grief to glee! said the bear.

When the cat came back inside, her mistress asked: – Pray tell me who would dare to knock and pad about past 9 o'clock?

– It's one of your suitors, replied the cat. – Go and talk to him, says he, and he will turn your grief to glee.

– What colour is his coat? asked the fox's widow.

– A fine fur of brown, said the maid. – Quite a size and the sharpest of eyes.

– Turn him away, turn him away! I will not hear what he has to say.

Coshe went over to the door, opened it just a crack and said:

– She says that I should turn you away, she will not hear what you have to say. So what else could the poor bear do but turn around and go back home.

The next Saturday evening someone knocked on the door again. This time there stood a wolf outside.

– Good evening, said the wolf. – Is the fox's widow at home? She certainly was.

– What is the widow doing this evening? Is she merry or is she grieving? he asked.

– Oh, she doesn't know which way to turn, answered the maid. – She's mourning because her dear husband is dead and crying so much her nose is quite red.

– Tell her she only need turn to me and I will soon turn her grief to glee, said the wolf.

– Pray tell me who would dare to knock and lope about past 9 o'clock? asked the fox's widow.

– Oh, it's just one of your suitors, said the cat. – Go and talk to

him, says he, and he will turn your grief to glee.

But first the fox's widow wanted to know what colour his coat was. – A fine fur of grey; long and sleek, slim but not weak, Coshe replied.

– Turn him away, turn him away! I will not hear what he has to say, said the widow. Now when the wolf heard this, what else could he do but turn around and go back home.

The third Saturday evening it happened again. There were three knocks on the door, and the cat went out to see who it was. On the doorstep stood a hare. – Good evening, he said.

– Likewise, she replied. – Are there strangers out a-visiting at this hour?

There certainly were. Then he too asked whether the fox's widow was home and what she was doing.

– She's mourning because her dear husband is dead and crying so much her nose is quite red, answered the maid.

– Tell her she only need turn to me and I will soon turn her grief to glee, said the hare.

– Pray tell me who would dare to knock and hop about past 9 o'clock? the widow asked Coshe.

– It's one of your suitors, I dare say, replied the maid.

Again her mistress wanted to know what colour his coat was.

– A fine fur of white; a beautiful sight, said the cat.

But it made no difference: – Turn him away, turn him away! I will not hear what he has to say, said the widow.

The fourth Saturday evening came. All at once there were three

knocks on the door. – Go and see who it is, said the widow to the maid. When the cat opened the door, there stood a fox on the doorstep.

– Good evening. It's a pleasure to meet you, said the fox.

– Pleasure to meet you, too, replied the maid.

– Is the widow at home? he asked.

– Yes, she's mourning because her dear husband is dead and crying so much her nose is quite red, answered the maid. – She doesn't know which way to turn, poor thing!

– Just tell her she only need turn to me and I will soon turn her grief to glee, said the fox.

Coshe went back inside. – Pray tell me who would dare to knock and dart about past 9 o'clock? asked her mistress.

– It's another of your suitors, to be sure, said the cat. – Go and talk to him, says he, and he will turn your grief to glee.

– What colour is his coat? asked the fox's widow.

– A fine fur of red, just like the one who's dead, answered the cat.

– Quick now, go invite him in,
I'm sure that I can turn to him! said the widow.

– Go and fetch my pretty socks, I'd like to meet this gallant fox;
Go and fetch my finest shoes, He's the one that I shall choose.

Yes, he was the one she wanted, and guests were invited to the wedding at the widow's cottage without a moment's delay. And unless he too has been to the farmer's henhouse, they are still living in Fox Cottage to this very day.

The Three Billy Goats Gruff

Once upon a time there were three billy goats, who were to go up to the hillside to make themselves fat, and the name of all three was Gruff.

On the way there was a bridge over a stream which they had to cross, and under the bridge lived a big, ugly troll with eyes as big as pewter plates and a nose as long as a rake handle.

First came the youngest Billy Goat Gruff to cross the bridge.

Clip-clap, clip-clap! *went the bridge.*

– Who's that clip-clapping over my bridge? roared the troll.

– Oh, it's only me, the smallest Billy Goat Gruff. I'm going up to the hillside to make myself fat, said the billy goat in a very small voice.

– Now I'm coming to get you, said the troll.

– Oh no, don't take me. I'm so little. Wait until the second Billy Goat Gruff comes; he's much bigger.

– Very well, then, said the troll. – Off with you.

A little while later came the second Billy Goat Gruff to cross the bridge.

Clip-clap, clip-clap, clip-clap! *went the bridge.*

– Who's that clip-clapping over my bridge? roared the troll.

– Oh, it's the second Billy Goat Gruff, and I'm going up to the hillside to make myself fat, said the billy goat, who hadn't such a small voice.

– Now I'm coming to get you, said the troll.

– Oh no, don't take me. Wait a little until the big Billy Goat Gruff comes, he's much, much bigger.

– Very well, then, said the troll. – Off with you.

Just then came the big Billy Goat Gruff.

Clip-clap, clip-clap, clip-clap! went the bridge, for the billy goat was so heavy that the bridge creaked and groaned under him.

– Who's that clip-clapping over my bridge? roared the troll.

– I'm the big Billy Goat Gruff, said the billy goat, who had a deep, gruff voice.

– Now I'm coming to get you! roared the troll.

– Come on then! I've got two spears,
    With them I'll pierce out your eyes and your ears!
    I've got as well two great, big stones,
    With them I'll crush your marrow and bones!

said the billy goat. And so he flew at the troll and stabbed out his eyes, and battered his marrow and bones, and butted him out into the stream. And then he went up to the hillside. There the billy goats got so fat that they could hardly walk home again. And if the fat hasn't come off them yet, why they're still fat.

And clip-clap-clop, here the tale must stop.

Little Freddie and his Fiddle

Once upon a time there was a farmer whose only son was so weak and in such poor health that he wasn't able to go to work. His name was Freddie and, because he was so small, they called him Little Freddie.

As there was so little food at home, his father went around the countryside to hire him out as a shepherd or errand boy. But no one wanted the boy, until he came to the sheriff. He was quite ready to take him, for he had just dismissed his errand boy and could not get another, as he was known to be a rogue. Something was better than nothing, thought the farmer. The boy was to earn his keep there, but nothing was said about wages or clothes. When Little Freddie had been there for three years, he wanted to leave, so the sheriff paid him all his wages at once: a penny for each year. – It couldn't be less, said the sheriff. So he got three pennies altogether.

Little Freddie thought that was a big sum, for he had never owned so much. Nevertheless, he asked if he might get a little more.

– You have got more than you ought to have, said the sheriff.

– Shouldn't I have anything for clothes, then? asked Little Freddie. – Those I had when I came are all worn out, and I haven't got any others. He was so ragged by this point, and his clothes hung in tatters and flapped about him.

– As you have got what we agreed on and three pennies besides, said the sheriff, – I'll have nothing more to do with you.

Little Freddie was, however, allowed to go out to the kitchen and put a little food in his knapsack, after which he left on the road to town to buy some clothes. He was as happy as a lark, for he had never seen a penny before. And every now and then he felt in his pockets to make sure all three were still there.

When he had gone far and farther than far, he came to a narrow valley with such high mountains all around that he could not see any way out, and he wondered what there might be on the other side of the mountains, and how he could ever get over them.

But he had to go up, so he set out. As he did not have much strength, he had to take rests from time to time, during which he counted his money. When he reached the very top, he found nothing but a great plain, overgrown with moss. There he sat down to see if he had all his pennies, when all of a sudden a poor man stood before him, and he was so big and tall that the boy began to scream when he saw how big and tall he really was.

– Don't be afraid, said the poor man, – for I won't hurt you. I only beg you, in God's name, for a penny.

– Oh dear! said the boy. – I've only got three pennies, and I was going to town to buy clothes with them.

– I'm worse off than you are, said the poor man, – for I have none at all, and I am even more ragged than you.

– Well, then, I guess you'll have to have it, said the boy.

After he had walked for a while, he was so tired that he sat down again to rest. Looking up, there he saw another poor man, even bigger and uglier than the first, and when the boy saw how tall and ugly he really was, he began to scream.

– Don't be afraid of me, said the poor man. – I won't hurt you. I only beg you, in God's name, for a penny.

– Oh dear, oh dear! said the boy. – I've only got two pennies, and I was going to town to buy clothes with them. If I'd only met you sooner, then...

– I'm worse off than you are, said the poor man. – I have no penny at all and a bigger body and less clothing.

– Well, then, I think I must let you have it, said the boy.

So he walked a while again, until he was tired, and then he sat down to rest. But no sooner had he sat down when again a poor man came up to him. He was so big and ugly and tall that the boy had to look up and up, until he was looking up to heaven, and when he saw how ugly and ragged the man really was, the boy began to scream.

– Don't be afraid of me, my good boy, said the man. – I won't hurt you, for I'm only a poor man who begs for a penny in God's name.

– Oh dear, dear! said Little Freddie. – I've only one penny left, and I was going to town to buy clothes with it. If I'd only met you sooner, then...

– Well, I have no penny at all, said the poor man, – and a bigger body and less clothing, so I'm worse off than you.

– Then I guess you'll have to take the penny, said Little Freddie. There was no way out of it, but it meant that each man had a penny and he had none.

– Well, since you have such a good heart, said the poor man,
–that you've given away all you owned, I'll give you a wish for each
penny. For it was the very same poor man who had got all three
pennies, and he had only changed himself each time so that the boy
could not recognize him.

– I've always had such a longing to hear the sound of a fiddle
and see people so merry and happy that they danced, said the boy.
– So, if I could wish for what I'd like, then I'd wish for a fiddle that
would make everything alive dance to its music.

– That you may have, said the man, – but that was a poor wish.
You ought to wish for something better with the other two pennies.

– I've always wanted to hunt and shoot, said Little Freddie, – so,
if I could wish for anything I'd like, I'd wish for a gun that would
make me hit everything I aimed at, be it ever so far off.

That was granted, too, but the man thought it was a poor wish.
– You must really wish for something better with the last penny, he
said.

– I have always wanted to be in company with good,
kind-hearted people, said Little Freddie, – so if I could wish for
anything I'd like, then I would wish that no one could deny me the
first thing I asked for.

– That wish wasn't such a bad one, said the poor man, and off
he hurried, disappearing into the hills. The boy lay down to sleep,
and the next day he came down from the mountains with his fiddle
and his gun.

First he went to the shopkeeper and asked for clothes, and then *at one farm he asked for a horse, and at another he asked for a sleigh, and at one place he wanted a fur coat, and no one could say No to him. No matter how stingy they were, they had to give him whatever he asked for. Finally he went about the countryside like a fine gentleman, with both horse and sleigh. After he had travelled for a while, he met the sheriff for whom he had worked.*

– Good day, master, said Little Freddie, stopping and lifting his hat.

– Good day, said the sheriff, – but have I ever been your master?

– Yes, don't you remember that I worked for you for three years for three pennies? said Little Freddie.

– My goodness! Then you have made good in no time! said the sheriff. – How on earth have you become such a fine gentleman?

– Oh, that's a long story, said the little fellow.

– Are you such a jolly fellow that you carry a fiddle about with you? asked the sheriff.

– Yes, I have always longed to make people dance, said the boy, – but the finest thing I've got is this gun. I shoot down almost everything I aim at, no matter how far off it is. Do you see the magpie sitting over there on the spruce tree? What do you bet that I can't hit it from here?

The sheriff did not mind betting, nor even to putting up his horse and farm and a hundred dollars besides, that Little Freddie could not hit the magpie. He was even willing to bet every cent he had on him, and fetch the bird when it fell. The sheriff did not believe there was a gun that could shoot that far. But bang went the gun, and down fell the magpie into a brier patch, and the sheriff rushed all the way in to fetch it, picked it up, and gave it to the boy. At that moment Little Freddie began to play his fiddle, and the sheriff danced till the thorns scratched him. He played on, and the sheriff danced and cried and begged for mercy, while his clothes flew about him in rags, till he had scarcely a thread left on his back.

– Well, now I think you're as ragged as I was when I left your service, said the boy, – so now I'll let you off. But first the sheriff had to pay what he had bet that the boy could not hit the magpie.

When the boy came to town, he went to an inn. There he played on his fiddle, and all who came danced, and he lived happily and well. He had no cares, for no one could deny him anything he asked for. But one day, when the fun was in full swing, the watchmen came to drag him off to the town hall, for the sheriff had entered a complaint against him, saying the boy had waylaid him and robbed him and almost taken his life. And now he was to be hanged, there was no way out of it. But Little Freddie knew a way out of everything, and that was with his fiddle. He began playing, and the watchmen had to dance till they lay there gasping. Then soldiers were sent in, but they fared no better than the watchmen. As soon as Little Freddie took up his fiddle, they had to dance as long as he could play, but they were worn out long before that.

Finally one night they sneaked in on him and seized him when he was asleep. And when they had him fast, he was sentenced to be hanged at once, and they lost no time in taking him to the gallows. A crowd of people came to see the spectacle. The sheriff was there, too, as happy as a lark, to get even for the money and the skin he had lost, and to watch them hang the boy. Things went rather slowly, for Little Freddie was quite feeble when it came to walking and pretended to be more feeble than ever. He had his gun and his fiddle along, too, for no one could get them away from him. And when he came to the gallows and had to climb up, he stopped and rested on every rung of the ladder. He sat down when he got to the last one and asked if they would grant him just one last favour. He wanted very much to play a tune on his fiddle before they hanged him. It would be indeed a sin and a shame to deny him that much, they said. But the sheriff begged them for heaven's sake not to let him touch a string, or else it would be the end of them all. If they let the boy play, why, as for himself, they'd have to tie him to the nearest birch tree.

It did not take Little Freddie long to get a jig out of his fiddle, and everyone and every living thing there began to dance, both those who went on two legs and those who went on four, parson and deacon and clerk and tramp and sheriff and masters and dogs and pigs. They danced and they laughed and screamed all at the same time. Some danced till they dropped, and others danced till they fainted. They all fared badly, but the sheriff worst of all, for he was tied to the birch tree and rubbed the skin all off his back as he danced. No one thought of doing anything to Little Freddie. They let him go wherever he pleased with his fiddle and gun, and he lived merrily for the rest of his days, for no one could say No to anything he asked for.

The Seventh Father of the House

Once upon a time there was a man who was travelling about, and he came at last to a big and beautiful farm. It was such a fine manor house that it might well have been a small castle. – This will be a good place to rest, said the man to himself as he came inside the gate. Nearby there was an old man with grey hair and beard, chopping wood. – Good evening, father, said the traveller. – Can I get lodgings here tonight?

– I'm not the father of the house, said the old man. – Go into the kitchen and speak to my father.

The traveller went into the kitchen. There he met a man who was still older, down on his knees in front of the hearth, blowing on the fire. – Good evening, father! Can I get lodgings here tonight? asked the traveller.

– I'm not the father of the house, said the old man. – But go in and speak to my father. He's sitting by the table in the next room.

So the traveller went into the room and spoke to the man who was sitting by the table. He was much older than the other two, and he sat there shivering and shaking, with chattering teeth, reading in a big book, almost like a little child. – Good evening, father! Can you give me lodgings here tonight? asked the man.

– I'm not the father of the house. But speak to my father over there, the one sitting on the bench, said the man who sat by the table with chattering teeth, shaking and shivering.

So the traveller went to the man who was sitting on the bench. He was trying to fill his pipe, but he was so huddled over and his hands shook so much that he was barely able to hold the pipe.

— Good evening, father, said the traveller again. — Can I get lodgings here tonight?

— I'm not the father of the house, said the old, huddled-over man. — But speak to my father, who is lying in the bed.

The traveller went to the bed, and there lay an old, old man, and the only thing about him that seemed to be alive was a pair of big eyes. – Good evening, father! Can I get lodgings here tonight? asked the traveller.

– I'm not the father of the house. But speak to my father, who is lying in the cradle, said the man with the big eyes.

So the traveller went to the cradle. There was a very, very old man lying, so shrunken, that he was not bigger than a baby, and one could not have known that there was life in him if it had not been for a sound coming from his throat now and then. – Good evening, father! Can I get lodgings here tonight? asked the man.

It took a long time before he got an answer, and still longer before the man had finished it. He said, like the others, that he was not the father of the house. – But speak to my father. He is hanging up in the horn on the wall there.

The traveller stared round the walls, and at last he caught sight of the horn. But when he looked for someone in it, there was scarcely anything to be seen but a little ash-white form, which had the appearance of a man's face. He was so frightened that he cried out loud: – Good evening, father! Will you give me lodgings here tonight?

There came a squeaking sound from the horn like a tom-tit, but it was just loud enough that he could make out that it meant: – Yes, my child.

And then a table came in, covered with the costliest dishes, and with ale and brandy. And when he had eaten and drunk, in came a good bed covered with reindeer skins, and the traveller was very glad that he at last had found the right father of the house.

White Bear King Valemon

Once upon a time there was, as there often is, a king. He had two daughters who were ugly and mean, but the third was as fair and sweet as the bright day, and the king and everyone was fond of her.

One day she dreamt of a golden wreath that was so lovely she couldn't live without it. But as she could not get it, she grew sullen and so sad she couldn't speak. When the king found out that it was the wreath she longed for, he sent out a likeness of the one that the princess had dreamt of to goldsmiths in every land, asking if they could make one like it. So the goldsmiths worked night and day, but some of the wreaths she threw away, and others she wouldn't even look at. One day, when she was in the forest, she caught sight of a white bear who had the very wreath she had dreamt of between his paws, and was playing with it. She wanted to buy it. No, it was not for sale for money, but she could have it if he could have her. Well, it was never worth living without it, she said. It didn't matter where she went or who she got, if only she could have the wreath. And so it was settled between them that he was to fetch her when three days were up, and that day was a Thursday.

When she came home with the wreath, everyone was glad because she was happy again. The king said it could not be very difficult to stop a white bear. On the third day the whole army was posted round the castle to fight him off. But when the white bear came, there was no one who could hold his ground against him, for no weapon could harm him, and he hurled soldiers down left and right, until they were lying in heaps. When the king saw how dreadfully things were going, he sent out his eldest daughter, and the white bear took her on his back and went off with her. When they had gone far and farther than far, the white bear asked: – Have you ever had a softer seat, and have you ever had clearer vision?

– Yes, my mother's lap was softer, and in my father's court my vision was clearer, she said.

– Oh, then you're not the right one, said the white bear and chased her home again.

The next Thursday he came back, and it all went the same as before. The army was out to fight off the white bear. But neither iron nor steel could go in him, and so he mowed them down like grass until the king begged him to stop. Then he sent out his next eldest daughter, and the white bear took her on his back and went off with her. When they had travelled far and farther than far, the white bear asked: – Have you ever had clearer vision, and have you ever had a softer seat?

– Yes, in my father's court my vision was clearer, and my mother's lap was softer, she said.

– Oh, then you're not the right one, said the white bear and with that he chased her home again.

On the third Thursday he came again. This time he fought harder than he had done before. The king felt that he couldn't let the bear slay his whole army, so he gave him his third daughter in God's name. He took her up on his back and went far and farther than far away. When they had reached the forest, he asked her, as he had asked the others, whether she had ever had a softer seat or clearer vision? – No, never! she said.

– Ah! You are the right one, he said.

They came to a castle which was so grand that the one her father had was like the poorest cottage in comparison. There she was to stay and live happily, and she was to have nothing else to do but to see that the fire never went out. The bear was away during the day, but at night he was with her, and then he was a man. For three years all went well. But each year she had a baby, and he took it and carried it off as soon as it had come into the world. Then she became more and more downhearted, and asked if she could go home and see her parents. Well, there was no objection to that. But first she had to give her word that she would listen to what her father said, but not to what her mother wished. So she went home. When they were alone with her, and she had told them how she was getting on, her mother wanted to give her a candle to take back so she could see what he looked like. But her father said: – No, she mustn't do that. It will do more harm than good. But regardless of whether it was good or not, she took the piece of candle with her when she left. The first thing she did when he had fallen asleep, was to light the candle and shine it on him. He was so handsome that she thought she could never gaze at him enough. But as she held the candle over him, a hot drop of tallow dropped on his forehead, and he woke up. – What have you done? he said. – Now you have made us both ill-fated. There was no more than a month left, and if you had only held out, I would have been saved. For a troll hag has cast

a spell over me, and I am a white bear by day. But now it is all over with us, for now I must go to her and take her to be my wife.

She wept and moaned. But he had no choice, he had to set off. Then she asked if she might go with him. – No, he said, that was out of the question. But when he set off in his bewitched bear form, she seized hold of the fur and threw herself up on his back, and held on fast. So away they went over crags and mountains, and through groves and thickets until her clothes were torn off her, and she was so dead tired that she let go her hold and fainted. When she came to, she was in a great forest, and she set off again, but she could not tell where the path led. After a long, long time she came to a cottage, and there she saw two women, an old woman and a pretty little girl. The princess asked if they had seen anything of White Bear King Valemon.

– Yes, he passed by here early this morning, but he went so fast you'll never be able to catch up with him, they said.

The little girl ran about clipping in the air and playing with a pair of golden scissors. Pieces of silk and strips of velvet flew all about her whenever she clipped in the air with them. Where they were, there was never any want of clothes.

– But this woman who is to travel so far and on such rough roads, she'll have to struggle hard, said the little girl, – she may well have more need of these scissors than I to cut her clothes with. May I give them to her? She was told she could.

So away travelled the princess through the forest, which seemed never to come to an end, both day and night, and the next morning *she came to another cottage. In it there were also two women, an old wife and a young girl. – Good day! said the princess. – Have you seen anything of White Bear King Valemon?*

– Was it you, maybe, who was to have him? asked the old wife. Yes, it was. – Well, he passed by yesterday, but he went so fast you'll never be able to catch up with him.

The little girl was playing about on the floor with a flask, which poured out whatever they wanted, and where it was, there was never any want of drink. – But this poor woman, said the girl, – who has to travel so far on such rough roads, I think she may well be thirsty and suffer many other hardships. No doubt she needs this flask more than I. May I give it to her? She was told she could.

So the princess got the flask, and thanked them, and set off again away through the same forest, both that day and the next night too. The third morning she came to a cottage, and there too she found an old wife and a little girl. – Good day! said the princess.

– Good day to you, said the old wife.

– Have you seen anything of White Bear King Valemon? she asked.

– Maybe it was you who was to have him? said the old wife. Yes, it was. – Well, he passed by here yesterday evening, but he went so fast you'll never be able to catch up with him, she said.

The little girl was playing about on the floor with a cloth which, when they said to it: – Cloth, spread yourself out and be covered with every good dish, it did so. And wherever it was, good food was never lacking. – But this poor woman, said the little girl, – who has to travel so far and on such rough roads, she may well starve and suffer many other hardships, so she'll have far more need of this cloth than I. May I give it to her? She was told she could.

So the princess took the cloth and thanked them, and set off again far and farther than far, away through the same dark forest all that day and night, and in the morning she came to a mountain spur, which rose into the sky like a huge wall, and so high and wide that she could see no end to it. There was a cottage too, and as soon as she set her foot inside it, she said: – Good day! Have you seen White Bear King Valemon pass this way?

– Good day to you, said the old wife. – It was you, maybe, who was to have him? Yes, it was. – Well, he passed by and went up over the mountain three days ago. But you can't get up there unless you have wings.

The cottage was packed with small children, and they all clung to their mother's skirt and cried for food. Then the old wife put a pot full of small round pebbles on the fire. When the princess asked what it was for, the wife said they were so poor they had neither food nor clothing, and it broke her heart to hear the children screaming for a bit to eat. But when she put the pot on the fire, and said: – The apples will soon be done, the words dulled their hunger, and they were patient for a while.

It was not long before the princess got out the cloth and the flask, as you can imagine. And when the children were all full and happy, she clipped out clothing for them with her golden scissors.

– Well, said the old wife, – since you have been so kind and

good to me and my children, it would be a shame if I didn't do all in my power to try to help you over the hill. My husband is really a master smith. Now you just rest until he comes back. I'll get him to forge you claws for your hands and feet, and then you can see if you can climb up.

When the smith came home, he set to work at once on the claws, and the next morning they were ready. She had no time to stay, so she took her leave, and then clung close to the rock and crept and crawled with the steel claws all that day and the next night. And just as she felt so very, very tired that she thought she could scarcely lift her hand again, and felt she would sink to the ground, she reached the top. There she found a plain, with tilled fields and meadows, so big and wide, she never thought there could be any land so wide and so flat. And close by there was a castle full of workmen of all kinds, who toiled like ants on an anthill.

– What is going on here? asked the princess. Well, they told her, there lived the troll hag who had cast a spell on White Bear King Valemon, and in three days she was to hold her wedding with him. The princess asked if she could speak with her. Of course not! That was out of the question! So she sat down outside the window and began to clip in the air with her golden scissors, and velvet and silken clothing flew about like a snow flurry.

When the troll hag saw that, she wanted to buy the scissors, for she said: – No matter how much the tailors toil, it's no use; we have too many to find clothes for. The scissors were not for sale for money, the princess said, but she could have them if she would let her sleep beside her sweetheart that night. Yes, she could certainly do that, said the troll hag, but she would lull him to sleep herself, and wake him in the morning. When he had gone to bed, she gave him a sleeping potion so he could not wake up, no matter how much the princess shouted and cried.

The next day the princess went outside the windows again, and began to pour something to drink from her flask. It flowed like a brook with beer and wine, and it was never empty. So when the troll hag saw that, she wanted to buy it, for no matter how much they toiled at the brewery and distillery, it was no use. They had too many to find drink for, she said. It was not for sale for money, the princess said, but if she would let her sleep beside her sweetheart that night, she could have it. Well, she could certainly do that, said the troll hag, but she would lull him to sleep herself, and wake him in the morning. When he had gone to bed, she gave him another sleeping potion, so the princess had no better luck that night, either. He couldn't be awakened no matter how much she cried and shouted. But that night one of the workmen was working in the room next to theirs. He heard the crying and understood what was going on. The next day he told the prince that she must have come, the princess who was to set him free.

That day the same thing happened with the cloth as with the scissors and the flask. When it was about dinner time, the princess went outside the castle, took out the cloth and said: – Cloth, spread yourself out and be covered with every good dish, and there was food enough for a hundred men. But the princess sat down to eat by herself. So when the troll hag set her eyes on the cloth, she wanted to buy it, for no matter how much they cooked and baked, it was no use. They had too many mouths to feed, she said. The princess said it was not for sale for money, but if she would let her sleep beside her sweetheart that night, she could have it. She could certainly do that, said the troll hag, but she would first lull him to sleep herself, and wake him up in the morning. When he had gone to bed, she came with the sleeping potion, but this time he was on his guard and fooled her. But the troll hag did not trust him one bit, for she took a darning needle and stuck it through his arm to see if he was sleeping soundly enough. But no matter how much it hurt, he did not stir a bit, and so the princess was allowed to come in to him.

Everything was going very well. Now if they could only get rid of the troll hag, he would be free. So he got the carpenters to make him a trick plank on the bridge over which the bridal procession had to pass, for it was the custom there that the bride rode at the head of the procession. When they got onto the bridge, the trick plank turned over on the bride and all the other old hags who were her bridesmaids. But King Valemon and the princess and all the rest of the wedding guests turned back to the castle and took away all they could carry of the troll hag's gold and money, and they set off for his land to hold their proper wedding. But on the way King Valemon picked up the three little girls and took them with them. And now she found out why he had taken her children away: it was so that they could help her find him. And at their wedding all ate and drank and made merry and were very happy.

The Princess who Couldn't be Silenced

Once upon a time there was a king. He had a daughter who was so wayward and willful in her speech that no one could silence her. The king therefore promised that the one who could outwit her would get the princess and half the kingdom in the bargain as well.

There were many who wanted to try, you may be sure, for it isn't every day that one can get a king's daughter and half a kingdom so easily. The gate to the king's manor hardly ever stood still. They came in great numbers from east and west, on horseback and on foot. But there was no one who could make the princess stop talking. At last the king announced that those who tried and failed would be branded on both ears with the great branding iron. He would not have all this running about the manor for nothing.

There were three brothers who had also heard about the princess, and as they were not so well off at home, they wanted to go out to try their luck and see if they could win the princess and half the kingdom. They were good friends and so they agreed to set out together. After they had gone a little way down the road, Askeladden found a dead magpie.

– Look what I've found! Look what I've found! he shouted.

– What have you found? asked the brothers.

– I have found a dead magpie, he said.

– Ugh! Throw it away! What can you do with that? said the other two, who always believed they were the wisest.

– Oh, I've nothing better to do, and nothing better to carry, so I'll just take it along with me, said Askeladden.

When they had gone a little bit further, Askeladden found an old birch binding, which he picked up.

– Look what I've found! Look what I've found! he shouted.

– What have you found now? said the brothers.

– I have found a birch binding, he replied.

– Pooh! What are you going to do with that? Throw it away! said the other two.

– Oh, I've nothing better to do, and nothing better to carry, so I'll just take it along with me, said Askeladden.

When they had gone still further, he found a piece of a broken saucer, which he also picked up. – See here boys! Look what I've found! Look what I've found! he said.

– Well, what have you found now? asked the brothers.

– A piece of a broken saucer, he said.

– Aargh! Now that's really worthless! Throw it away! they said.

– Oh, I've nothing better to do, and nothing better to carry, so I'll just take it along with me, said Askeladden.

When they had gone a little bit further, he found a twisted goat horn and soon after he found the mate to it. – Look what I've found! Look what I've found, boys! he shouted.

– What have you found now? asked the others.

– Two goat horns, answered Askeladden.

– Aargh! Throw them away! What are you going to do with them? they said.

– Oh, I've nothing better to do, and nothing better to carry, so I'll just take it along with me, said Askeladden.

After a while he found a wedge. – Hey! See here boys! Look what I've found! Look what I've found! he shouted.

– There's no end to what you find! What have you found now? asked the two eldest.

– I have found a wedge, he answered.

– Oh, throw it away! What are you going to do with that?

– Oh, I've nothing better to do, and nothing better to carry, so I'll just take it along with me, said Askeladden.

As they went across the fields by the king's manor where manure had recently been spread, he bent down and picked up a worn-out shoe sole. – Hey boys! Look what I've found! Look what I've found! he shouted.

– If only you could find a little more sense by the time you got there! said the other two. – What is it you have found now?

– A worn-out shoe sole, he replied.

– Ugh! What an awful thing to pick up! Throw it away! What are you going to do with it? asked the brothers.

– Oh, I've nothing better to do, and nothing better to carry, so I'll just take it along with me, if I'm to win the princess and half the kingdom, said Askeladden.

– Yes, you're likely to do that, you are! said the other two.

They were let in to see the princess. The eldest went first.

– Good day! he said.

– Good day to you! she answered with a squirm.

– It's terribly warm in here, he said.

– It's warmer in the coals, the princess answered. The branding iron was lying waiting in the coals. When he saw the branding iron, he was struck speechless, and it was all over for him.

The second brother fared no better. – Good day! he said.

– Good day to you, she said with a wriggle.

– It's terribly hot in here, he said.

– It's hotter in the coals, she replied. With that he too lost both speech and wits, and the iron had to be brought out again.

Then came Askeladden. – Good day! he said.

– Good day to you! she replied with a squirm and a wriggle.

– It's very nice and warm in here! said Askeladden.

– It's warmer in the coals, she answered. She was in no better mood now with the third one.

– There's a chance for me to roast my magpie on it, then? he asked.

– I'm afraid she will burst, said the princess.

– No fear of that! I'll tie this birch binding round her, he said.

– It will be too wide, she said.

– I'll drive in a wedge, said the boy, and brought out the wedge.

– The fat will run off her, said the king's daughter.

– Then I'll hold this under it, said the lad, and showed her the piece of the broken saucer.

– Your words are so twisted, said the princess.

– No, my words aren't twisted, but this is twisted, answered the boy, and took out one of the goat horns.

50

– Well, I've never seen the like! shouted the princess.

– Here you see the like, said the lad and took out the other one.

– It seems you've become worn out trying to get the better of me, she said.

– No, I'm not worn out, but this is, answered the lad, and pulled out the shoe sole.

And with that the princess was silenced.

– Now you are mine! said Askeladden, and so he got her and half the kingdom in the bargain.

The Boy and the Devil

Once upon a time there was a boy who went along a road cracking nuts. He came upon a worm-eaten one, and just then he met the devil.

– Is it true what they say, said the boy, – that the devil can make himself as small as he likes, and go through a pin-prick?

– Yes, answered the devil.

– Let me see you creep into this nut, then, said the boy. And the devil did so. But as soon as the devil had crept in through the wormhole, the boy pushed a twig into it. – Now I've got you, he said, and put the nut in his pocket.

Further along the road he came to a smithy. He went in there and asked the smith if he would crack that nut for him.

– Yes, that's easily done, said the smith, and took the smallest hammer he had, laid the nut on the anvil and hit it, but the nut wouldn't crack. So he took a somewhat bigger hammer, but that wasn't heavy enough either. Then he took an even bigger one, but the nut still would not crack. This made the smith angry, and he seized the big sledgehammer. – This time I'll crack you! he said, and swung with all his might. The nut burst into splinters with such a roaring crash that half the roof blew off the smithy, and it sounded as though the entire shed would come crashing down.

– I think the devil was in that nut! said the smith.

– He was! replied the boy.

Askeladden and the Good Helpers

Once upon a time there was a king who had heard of a ship that went just as fast on land as on water, and he wanted to have one like it. So he promised his daughter and half the kingdom to anyone who could build him a ship like that. He proclaimed this in all the churches throughout the land. There were many who tried, you may be sure, for half the kingdom would be good to have, they thought, and the king's daughter would be fine to have in the bargain as well. Nevertheless, they all failed.

Now there were three brothers who lived in a village in the woods. The eldest was called Per, the next one Paul and the youngest was called Espen Askeladden, because he was always poking and raking in the ashes. On the Sunday when the proclamation about the ship the king wanted was read, Askeladden happened to be there. When he came home and told the others about it, Per, the eldest, asked his mother for some provisions, for he wanted to go off and try his luck at building the ship, and winning the king's daughter and half the kingdom.

No sooner he had got his knapsack of provisions on his back than he was off. On his way he met a bent, wretched-looking old man. – Where are you off to? asked the man.

– I'm going to the forest to make a trough for my father. He doesn't like to eat with the rest of us, said Per.

– Trough it'll be! said the man. – What've you got in your knapsack?

– Dung! said Per.

– Dung it'll be! said the man.

So off went Per into the oak forest and chopped and built with all his might and main. But no matter how hard he chopped, and how much he built, he could produce nothing but troughs and more troughs. When it came to dinner time, he was going to have something to eat, and he opened the knapsack. There was something in the sack, but it sure wasn't food! Since he had nothing to eat, and no success with his work, he got tired of it all, put the axe and the knapsack on his back, and went home to his mother.

Then Paul wanted to set out, and try his luck at building the ship and winning the king's daughter and half the kingdom. He asked his mother for provisions, and when he had got them, he set out for the forest. On his way he met a bent, wretched-looking old man.

– Where are you off to? asked the man.

– Oh, I'm off to the forest to make a trough for our little pig, said Paul.

– Pig trough it'll be! said the man. – What have you got in your sack?

– Dung! said Paul.

– Dung it'll be! said the man.

So off went Paul into the forest and started chopping and building as hard as he could. But no matter how hard he chopped, and how much he built, he could produce nothing but trough shapes and pig troughs. Just the same, he didn't give up, but carried on until late in the afternoon before he thought of having something

to eat. Then he was suddenly so hungry that he had to get out his knapsack. But when he came to open it, it was full of anything but food! Paul was so angry that he turned the sack inside out and flung it against a tree stump. Then he picked up his axe, left the forest and went straight home.

After Paul came home, Askeladden wanted to set out, and he asked his mother for provisions. – Maybe I could manage to get the ship built and win the king's daughter and half the kingdom, he said. – Yes, very likely! said his mother. – You who never do anything but root and rake in the ashes! No! I'm not going to give you any provisions. But Askeladden wouldn't give up. He pleaded so hard that in the end he was allowed to go. He got no provisions, though. But he did sneak along a couple of oatcakes and a drop of stale beer, and away he went.

After he had gone a little way, he met the same old fellow, the one who was so bent and pitiful and wretched-looking.

– Where are you off to? asked the man.

– Oh, I'm off to the forest to build a ship which goes just as well on land as on water, said Askeladden. – For the king has proclaimed that whoever can build such a ship will get the king's daughter and half the kingdom.

– What do you have in your sack? asked the man.

– Oh, it's not much to speak of. It's supposed to be provisions, replied Askeladden.

– If you'll give me a little of them, I'll help you, said the man.

– I would gladly, said Askeladden, – but it's no more than two *oatcakes and a drop of stale beer. That didn't matter said the old man. If only he got some of it, he would help.*

When they came to the old oak in the forest, the man said:
– Now you must cut out a piece of wood and put it back where it came from. After that you can lie down and go to sleep. Askeladden did as he was told. He lay down to sleep, and in his sleep he seemed to hear somebody chopping and hammering and building and sawing and joining. He could not wake up, however, before the man woke him. When at last he could open his eyes, there stood the ship, completely finished, alongside the oak. – Now you must get on board, and everyone you meet, you're to take with you, said the old man. Well, Espen Askeladden said he would do as the old man told him, and thanked him for the ship. Then he sailed away.

When he had sailed a little way, he came across a tall, skinny tramp who lay on a hillside eating lumps of granite. – What sort of a fellow are you to be lying here eating granite? asked Askeladden.

The man said he was so hungry for meat that he could never get his fill. That was why he had to eat granite. And then he asked if he could come along on the ship. – Sure, if you want to come along, climb aboard, said Askeladden. So the man came aboard, bringing some granite with him as provisions.

When they had sailed a bit farther, they met a fellow who was lying on a sunny hillside sucking on a barrel tap.

– What sort of a fellow are you? asked Espen Askeladden. – And what's the good of sucking on that barrel tap?

– If one hasn't a barrel, one must be satisfied with the tap. I'm

always so thirsty for beer that I can never drink enough beer or wine, he said, and asked if he could come along on the ship.

– If you want to come along, climb aboard, said Askeladden. So he climbed aboard, bringing with him the tap to quench his thirst.

When they had sailed a bit farther, they came across a man who was lying with one ear to the ground, listening.

– What sort of a fellow are you, and what are you listening to there on the hillside? asked Askeladden.

– I'm listening to the grass, for my hearing is so sharp that I can hear the grass growing, he said. And then he asked if he could come along on the ship.

– If you want to come along, climb aboard, said Askeladden. So he climbed aboard, too.

When they had sailed a bit farther, they came across a man who stood aiming a gun. – What sort of a fellow are you, and what's the good of standing and aiming like that? asked Askeladden.

– My sight is so good, he said, – that I can shoot straight to the world's end. Then he asked if he could come along on the ship.

– If you want to come along, climb aboard, said Askeladden. And so he climbed aboard, too.

When they had sailed a bit farther, they met a man who was hopping along on one leg, and on the other leg were fastened seven heavy weights.

– What sort of a fellow are you, and what's the good of hopping along on one leg with seven heavy weights on the other?

– I move so fast, he said, – that if I walked on both legs, I'd reach

the end of the world in less than five minutes. Then he asked if he could come along on the ship.

– If you want to come along, climb aboard, said Askeladden. So he climbed up into the ship to join Askeladden and his companions.

When they had sailed a bit farther, they met a man who was holding his hand over his mouth.

– What sort of a fellow are you, asked Askeladden, – and why are you holding your hand over your mouth like that?

– Oh, I've got seven summers and fifteen winters inside my body! he said. – So I have to hold my mouth shut, for if I let them all out at once, they would destroy the world right away. And then he asked if he could come along.

– If you want to come along, climb aboard, said Askeladden. So he climbed aboard the ship with the others.

When they had sailed a bit farther, they arrived at the king's manor. Askeladden went straight in to the king and said that the ship was standing ready outside, and now he wanted the king's daughter, just as the king had promised.

The king wasn't too pleased about this, for Askeladden looked both dirty and sooty, and the king was reluctant to give his daughter to such a tramp. So he said he'd have to wait a bit. He couldn't have the princess until he had emptied the royal meat store which contained three hundred barrels of meat. – If you can get it done by this time tomorrow, then you shall have her, said the king.

– Well, I'll try, said Askeladden, – if I can take one of my companions with me. He was told he could even take all six if he

liked, for the king thought the task was quite impossible even with as many as six hundred.

Askeladden only took with him the man who chewed granite, and was always so hungry for meat. When they came and unlocked the storehouse, he had eaten it all up, leaving only six small shoulders of salt mutton, one for each of the other companions.

Then Askeladden went in to the king and told him that the storehouse was empty, and now he had come for the king's daughter.

The king went to see for himself, and he found it empty. But Askeladden was still dirty and sooty, and the king thought it was really too bad that such a tramp should have his daughter. So he said he had a cellar full of beer and old wine, three hundred barrels of each kind, which he wanted cleared first. – And if you can drink it all up by this time tomorrow, then you shall have her, said the king.

– I'll try, said Askeladden, – if I can take one of my companions with me.

– Yes, certainly, said the king, thinking that he had so much beer and wine that there would be more than enough for all seven of them.

Askeladden took along the man who sucked on the tap and was always so thirsty for beer, and the king locked them both in the cellar. The man drank barrel after barrel as long as there was anything left. But in the very last one he left enough for his companions to have a mug or two.

In the morning when they opened the cellar door, out came

Askeladden who went straight to the king and said he had finished up the beer and the wine, and now he wanted the king's daughter, just as he had promised.

– Yes, but first I must go to the cellar and see, said the king, for of course he didn't believe it. When he got there, he found nothing but empty barrels. But Askeladden was still dirty and sooty, and the king felt it was unseemly to have such a son-in-law. So he said that if the boy could fetch water from the end of the world for the princess's tea in ten minutes, then he could get both her and half the kingdom. For that was certainly quite impossible, he believed.

– I'll try, said Askeladden. So he got hold of the one who hopped along on one leg and had seven heavy weights on the other, and told him to remove his weights and use both legs as fast as he could, for he had to have some water from the end of the world for the princess's tea in ten minutes!

The man took off the weights, got a bucket, and set off, and immediately he was out of sight. But time dragged on and on, seemingly forever, and he didn't come back. When there were only three minutes before the time was up, the king was as delighted as if he had been given a shilling.

But then Askeladden called the man who could hear the grass growing, and told him to listen to find out what had happened to him. – He has fallen asleep by the well, he said. – I can hear him snoring, and the trolls are stroking his head.

Then Askeladden called the one who could shoot straight to the end of the world, and asked him to put a bullet in the troll, which he did. He shot him right in the eye. The troll let out a roar so loud that it woke the man who had gone to fetch the tea water. And when he came back to the king's manor, there was still one minute of the ten left.

Askeladden went in to the king and presented him with the water, and said that now he wanted the king's daughter, and that surely this was to be the end of the matter. But the king thought he looked just as dirty and sooty as before, and he didn't want to have him for a son-in-law. So the king said that he had three hundred cords of wood with which he was going to dry the grain in the bathhouse. – And if you can manage to sit in there and burn it all up, then you shall have her, have no doubt, he said.

– I'll try, said Askeladden – if I can take one of my companions with me.

– Yes, take all six if you like, said the king, for he thought it would be hot enough for them all.

Askeladden took with him the man who had fifteen winters and seven summers in his body, and went into the bathhouse in the evening. The king had made it roaring hot in there. In fact, the heat was so great that they could easily have forged iron stoves in that bathhouse. They could not get out, for once they had come in, the king had bolted the door shut and put on a couple of extra padlocks as well. So Askeladden said: – You'll have to let out six or seven winters and get the temperature down to summer warmth. Then it grew comfortable enough for them to withstand it. Throughout the night, however, it became quite chilly. So Askeladden told him to warm it up a bit with a couple of summers, and then they slept till late in the day. But when they heard the king outside the door, Askeladden said: – Now you must let out a couple of more winters, but see to it that the last one catches him right in the face. He did just that, and when the king opened the door to the bathhouse, expecting to see them burnt to death, he found them sitting there shivering and freezing with their teeth chattering. The man with the fifteen winters in his body let the last one out right in the king's face, giving him frostbite.

– Do I get the king's daughter now? asked Askeladden.

– Yes, take her and keep her, and take the kingdom as well, said the king. He no longer dared refuse him. So at last the wedding was held, and Askeladden got his princess.

Butterball

Once upon a time there was a wife who was fond of baking. She had a little son, who was so round and fat and fond of good things, that she called him Butterball. She also had a dog called Goldtooth. One day Goldtooth suddenly began to bark. – Run out, my little Butterball, said the wife, – and see what Goldtooth is barking at. So the boy ran out, and came back and said: – Oh, heaven help me! Here comes a big, tall troll hag with her head under her arm, and a sack on her back! – Run under the breadboard and hide! said his mother.

The big troll came in. – Good day! she said.

– God bless you! said Butterball's mother.

– Is Butterball home today? asked the troll.

– No, he's out in the woods with his father bagging grouse, answered the mother.

– Oh, what a troll thing to happen! said the troll hag. – I've got a nice little silver knife I wanted to give him.

– Squeak! Squeak! Here I am! said Butterball from under the breadboard, and out he sprang.

– I'm so old and my back's so stiff, said the troll, – you must crawl into the sack and fetch it yourself. But when Butterball had crawled deep into the sack, the troll swung it on her back and rushed out the door. After they had gone a little way down the road, the troll grew tired and asked: – How far off is it to where I can sleep?

– Half a mile, answered Butterball.

So the troll put the sack down by the roadside, and went alone into the forest, and lay down to sleep. In the meantime, Butterball saw his chance. He took his knife, cut a hole in the sack, and jumped out. Then he put a large fir root into the sack, and ran home to his mother. When the troll got home and saw what there was in the sack, she flew into a dreadful rage.

*The next day the wife was baking again. Suddenly the dog
began to bark. – Run out, my little Butterball, she said, – and see
what Goldtooth is barking at. – Oh no! Oh no! It's that nasty beast
again, mother! said Butterball. – She's coming back with her head
under her arm and a big sack on her back!*

– Run under the breadboard and hide! said his mother.

– Good day! said the troll. – Is Butterball home today?

*– No, indeed he isn't, said his mother. – He's out in the woods
with his father bagging grouse.*

*– Oh, what a troll thing to happen! said the troll hag. – I've got
a beautiful little silver fork I wanted to give him.*

*– Squeak! Squeak! Here I am! said Butterball from under the
breadboard, and out he sprang.*

*– My back's so stiff, said the troll, – you must crawl into the sack
and fetch it yourself. But when Butterball had crawled deep into the
sack, the troll swung it on her back and set off. After they had gone
a little way down the road, she grew tired and asked:*

– How far off is it to where I can sleep?

– About a mile, answered Butterball.

*So the troll set the sack down by the side of the road, and went
alone into the forest, and lay down to sleep. While the troll took her
nap, Butterball made a hole in the sack, and once he was out, he put
a big stone into it. When the troll hag got home, she made a fire in
the hearth, and put a big pot on it, and was going to boil Butterball.
But when she took the sack, and thought she was going to turn out
Butterball into the pot, down fell the stone, making a hole in the*

bottom of the pot, so the water ran out and put out the fire. Then the troll became very angry and said: – No matter how heavy he makes himself next time, I'll trick him just the same, I will!

The third time the same thing happened again. Goldtooth began to bark, and Butterball's mother said to him: – Run out, my little Butterball, and see what Goldtooth is barking at.

Butterball ran out and came back saying:

– Oh, heaven help me! Here comes the troll again, with her head under her arm and a sack on her back!

– Run under the breadboard and hide! said his mother.

– Good day! said the troll, as she came in through the door. – Is Butterball home today?

– No, indeed he isn't, said his mother. – He's out in the woods with his father bagging grouse.

– Oh, what a troll thing to happen! said the troll hag. – I've got a beautiful little silver spoon I wanted to give him.

– Squeak! Squeak! Here I am! said Butterball from under the breadboard, and out he sprang.

– My back's so stiff, said the troll hag, – you must crawl into the sack and fetch it yourself. But when Butterball had crawled deep into the sack, the troll swung it on her back, and set off. This time she did not go off by herself to sleep, but went straight home with Butterball in the sack, and when they got there, it was a Sunday.

The troll said to her daughter: – Now, you must take Butterball and cut him up, and make broth of him till I come back again, for I'm going to church to invite some friends to a feast.

When all in the house had gone to church, the daughter was going to take Butterball and kill him, but she didn't quite know how to go about it. – Stop a bit, said Butterball. – I'll show you how to do it. Put your head on the stool, and you'll see.

So she did, poor thing, and Butterball took the axe and chopped her head off, just as if she had been a chicken. Then he put the head in the bed, and the body in the pot, and made broth of the troll hag's daughter. After he had done that, he climbed up over the door, and dragged the fir root and the stone with him, and put one over the door, and the other on the troll's chimney pipe.

When the other trolls came home from church and saw the head in the bed, they thought their daughter was asleep. Then they went to taste the broth.

– Tastes good, Butterball broth! said the troll hag.

– Tastes good, daughter broth! said Butterball, but no one heeded him.

Then the mountain troll took the spoon and was going to taste.

– Tastes good, Butterball broth! he said.

– Tastes good, daughter broth! said Butterball from his hiding place up on the chimney pipe.

Then they all began to wonder who was talking, and went to see. But when they got to the door, Butterball threw the fir root and the stone at their heads and killed them all. After that he took all the gold and silver in the house, and you can imagine how rich he became. Then he went home to his mother.

Photos: Ivo Caprino

This book is also available in
Norwegian: Asbjørnsen og Moes eventyrverden
                ISBN 82-7362-026-3
German: Norwegische Märchen
                ISBN 82-7362-029-8